A Note to Parents and Teachers

DK READERS is a compelling program for beginning readers, designed in conjunction with leading literacy experts.

Beautiful illustrations and superb full-color photographs combine with engaging, easy-to-read stories to offer a fresh approach to each subject in the series. Each DK READER is guaranteed to capture a child's interest while developing his or her reading skills, general knowledge, and love of reading.

The five levels of DK READERS are aimed at different reading abilities, enabling you to choose the books that are exactly right for your child:

Pre-level 1 – Learning to read
Level 1 – Beginning to read
Level 2 – Beginning to read alone
Level 3 – Reading alone
Level 4 – Proficient readers

The "normal" age at which a child begins to read can be anywhere from three to eight years old, so these levels are only a general guideline.

No matter which level you select, you can be sure that you are helping your child learn to read, then read to learn!

LONDON, NEW YORK, MUNICH,
MELBOURNE, AND DELHI

Editor Kate Simkins
Designer Cathy Tincknell
Art Director Mark Richards
Publishing Manager Simon Beecroft
Category Publisher Alex Kirkham
Production Rochelle Talary
DTP Designer Lauren Egan

For Lucasfilm
Art Editor Iain R. Morris
Senior Editor Jonathan W. Rinzler
Continuity Supervisor Leland Chee

Reading Consultant
Linda B. Gambrell, Professor and
Director, Eugene T. Moore School of
Education, Clemson University.

First American Edition, 2005
Published in the United States by
DK Publishing, Inc.
375 Hudson Street
New York, New York 10014

07 08 09 10 9 8 7 6 5

Published in Great Britain by Dorling Kindersley Limited.

A catalog record for this book is available from
the Library of Congress

ISBN-13: 978-0-7566-1158-3 (hb)
ISBN-13: 978-0-7566-1159-0 (pb)

Reproduced by Media Development and Printing Ltd., UK
Printed and bound in China by L. Rex Printing Co. Ltd.

Discover more at
www.dk.com

www.starwars.com

DK READERS

LUCAS BOOKS

STAR WARS™
Journey Through
SPACE

Written by Ryder Windham

BEGINNING
2
TO READ ALONE

DK

Come on a journey through space
to the *Star Wars* galaxy.
It is far, far away.
In this galaxy, there are
many stars and planets.

Coruscant (CORE-RUS-SANT)
is the most important planet.
It is covered by one enormous city.
All the buildings in the city
are gleaming skyscrapers.

Jedi Knights

Many creatures live in
the *Star Wars* galaxy.
Coruscant is the home
of powerful warriors
called Jedi Knights.

Yoda

People and Gungans live on
the planet Naboo.
The people live in beautiful cities
on the land.
Young Padmé Amidala was once
Queen of Naboo.

*Queen
Amidala*

The Gungans live
in underwater cities.
They can walk
on land too,
although some are
a bit clumsy!
Jar Jar Binks
is a Gungan.

*Jar Jar
Binks*

Podracing

Tatooine is famous
for Podracing.
In this dangerous sport,
fast vehicles race each
other through the desert.

The planet Tatooine (TA-TOO-EEN)
is covered by a dusty desert.
Two suns shine in the sky so
it is very hot.
Tatooine is a meeting place.
Space travelers visit the planet from
all over the galaxy.

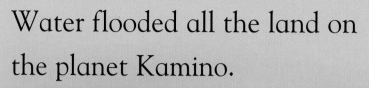

Water flooded all the land on
the planet Kamino.
So the Kaminoans built their cities
on strong metal poles that stick up
above the water.

Kaminoans are very tall
with long, thin necks.
They ride winged beasts
to fly and swim around
their watery planet.

Geonosis (GEE-OH-NO-SIS) is not a good place to be captured. Prisoners are forced to fight huge monsters in special arenas.

Huge arenas
The arenas are made of rock. There are lots of seats inside.

Scary beasts are brought from other planets to the arenas.
The Geonosians look like insects and enjoy watching the fights.

Chewbacca

Tarfful

Kashyyyk (KASH-ICK) is a world
of giant trees and shallow lakes.
It is home to the Wookiees,
including Chewbacca and Tarfful.
Wookiees are tall and have lots
of shaggy fur.
They talk in grunts and roars.

Good friends

Chewbacca is friends
with a human
called Han Solo.
They fly together
in a starship—the
Millennium Falcon.

The planet Utapau
(OO-TA-POW)
has lots of deep holes.
The Utapauns dig
tunnels through
the rocks to join
the holes.

There are other
creatures on
the planet.

An Utapaun

Creatures called
Utai (OO-TIE) live in
holes in the ground.

Enormous varactyl
(VA-RACK-TILL)
wander around
the rocky land.
They are good
climbers.

An Utai

The Utai ride the varactyl.

A varactyl

The red planet of Mustafar
(MUSS-TAH-FAR) is
a very hot place.
It is covered in fiery volcanoes.
Hot, melted rock called lava
flows from the volcanoes.
The sky is filled with black smoke
that blocks out the sun.

Fight on Mustafar

Two Jedi Knights, Obi-Wan Kenobi and Anakin Skywalker, fought each other on Mustafar. Anakin had turned from good to evil. Obi-Wan won the fight.

The space rock known as
Polis Massa (POE-LISS-MASS-AH)
has a medical center.
This is where space travelers can go
if they are sick.

The doctors are helped
by special robots
called droids.

Medical droid

Polis Massa doctors

Birth place

Padmé Amidala came to Polis Massa to give birth. She had twins.

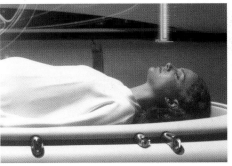

The moon Yavin 4 is covered
in thick jungle.
The ruins of very old buildings
called temples rise above the trees.

At one time, the soldiers
who lived on Yavin 4 kept watch
for enemy starships from
the tops of the tallest temples.

What's inside the temples?

The temples were once used to keep starships. There were also rooms where people could eat and sleep.

The ice planet Hoth
is so cold that people can
freeze to death there.

On Hoth, people ride around on
large beasts called tauntauns.

Wampa ice creatures
live in ice caves.
They hang
the animals that
they catch from
the cave roof.

One time, a wampa even captured
a Jedi Knight!

The planet Dagobah (DAY-GO-BA) is covered in thick forests and swampy land.

The air is steamy, and it rains a lot. There are many deadly creatures and poisonous plants.

The Jedi Master Yoda went
to hide on Dagobah.
He lived in a small tree house.

Crash landing

Young pilot
Luke Skywalker
crashed his
starship on
Dagobah.
Yoda found Luke
and took him to
his tiny house.

Cloud City floats in the skies of
the planet Bespin.

Visitors come to enjoy
its lively shops, restaurants,
and hotels.

A cloud car

Cloud cars fly around the city.
They have room for two passengers.

The forest moon of
the planet Endor is
the home of small, furry
creatures called Ewoks.
They live in the trees and
use simple tools and spears.

At night, Ewoks stay in the villages that they build high up in the trees.

We hope that you have enjoyed your trip to the *Star Wars* galaxy. Come back soon!

Fascinating facts

There are millions and millions of planets and suns in the enormous *Star Wars* galaxy.

Some of the skyscrapers on Coruscant are nearly a mile high.

The Queen of Naboo lives in the Royal Palace. This beautiful building has large windows and polished stone floors.

The trees on Kashyyyk are very tall. The Wookiees make houses in the trees.

The tauntauns have thick gray fur to protect them from the cold on Hoth.